THE PEACEABLE FOREST

INDIA'S TALE OF KINDNESS TO ANIMALS

KOSA ELY

Illustrations by Anna Johansson

INSIGHT KIDS
A MANDALA BOOK

San Rafael, California

Long ago, in a peaceful forest, the animals played together in the sunshine. An old man who lived in this forest called to them, "Come, gather 'round. I'll tell you a story, a story you've never heard before."

Animals love stories as much as children do. So they scampered in close and perked up their ears, eager to hear a new story.

"Once, not so long ago, a hunter lived in this very forest," the old man began. "This hunter didn't kill just to eat. He also killed for fun."

The animals gasped and huddled closer together.

"Your grandparents and great-grandparents lived in fear of him," the old man continued.

"The twang of his bow sent them running for their lives. One day something happened to change all that. . . ."

A holy man, a sage by the name of Narada, came through this forest, singing and strumming his vina.

The animals and birds followed the
sage, dancing and humming along.

Narada's singing stopped when he heard someone crying out in pain. He ran toward the sound and soon found a fawn, pierced with a hunter's arrow. Narada knelt down to comfort her and asked, "Do you know who has done this to you, my child?"

"Sage, please help me," said the fawn. "It was the hunter. I am too weak to run to my mother. She warned me to be careful, to stay hidden. But I wanted to eat the new grasses and flowers. I was gathering some for her when I was shot." The fawn added with a whisper, "Please stop him before he hurts my mother."

Overhead, a flock of birds guarded the fawn, and a messenger went to bring her mother.

"Sage, they will look after her," their leader, Chakor, said. "There are others who need you. Can you come with me?"

Chakor led Narada to a large boar who lay twisting in pain from the arrow in his side.

Seeing the sage, the boar nodded his head in respect, then said, "I don't know if you can help me, but please stop this hunter from killing anyone else. I have five young children. How will my wife keep them safe? As long as this hunter lives, all of them are in danger."

Hearing muffled crying, Narada turned to see five sets of eyes looking back at him.

"I will find this hunter," the sage told the boar, "and I'll come back to help you and your family."

Narada followed Chakor to a part of the forest where the sun shone brightly through the trees. There lay a wounded rabbit.

The rabbit told Narada, "My little brother plays games in the sunshine and forgets to look out for snakes and hawks. I stay near to protect him. I was hiding my brother from the hunter when he shot me."

"Do you know where this hunter is now?" Narada asked.

"He went that way," answered the rabbit, pointing with his nose.

Narada and Chakor moved ahead quickly and then stopped. The hunter stood behind a tree just a short distance away. He had an arrow fitted to his bow, ready to shoot again.

Narada ran to the hunter. Chakor cried out a warning for the animals to run and hide.

The hunter was angry. "Sage," he said, "why have you left the path and come to me?"

In a kind voice, Narada asked, "Do the arrows that have injured the deer, the boar, and the rabbit belong to you?"

"Yes!" the hunter said proudly. "Both the arrows and the animals I have shot are mine."

"Please tell me," the sage asked, "why are you causing them so much pain?"

"Why not?" challenged the hunter. "My name is Mrigari, which means 'enemy of animals.' My father taught me to hunt this way. I feel happy when animals feel pain. What difference does it make to you?"

"It will make a difference to you," Narada said. "Let me show you."

The sage lifted his arms. A strong wind
swept through the forest, whirling
the leaves. As they settled, the hunter
looked around him. Every animal he
had ever hurt or killed now surrounded
him—elephants, tigers, wolves, deer,
monkeys, rabbits, birds, and snakes.

"Look around at each of these animals, Mrigari,"
the sage said. "Remember the pain you caused them.
They will come back, one after another, life after life, to
find you. This is the future you have created for yourself."

The scene changed. Now hunters chased Mrigari and shot him with arrows. Mrigari first was a tiger, then a boar, then a deer. Over and over again, he felt the fear of being hunted and the pain of the arrows.

Something inside Mrigari began to change.

"The deer you shot today is just a child," Narada reminded him. "She was gathering new grasses and flowers for her mother when your arrow hit her.

"The boar has five young children to care for.

"The rabbit was watching out for his brother when you shot him."

"Stop!" Mrigari said. "How many animals have I killed? How many families have suffered because of me? No more. I won't kill any more."

Mrigari asked through his tears, "Sage, what can I do? How can I change?"

Narada waved his hand, and the visions disappeared. "There is a way," he said, "but you must be willing."

"I will do anything," Mrigari promised.

"Break your bow," Narada said. "From today on, never harm or eat another animal."

"But how will I live?" asked Mrigari. "What will I eat?"

"You do not have to kill to eat. The earth produces fruits and vegetables, grains and beans. You will not go hungry."

Clasping his prized bow with both hands, Mrigari bent the ends together. A loud crack echoed through the forest as the bow snapped in two. His life as a hunter was over, and he sighed with relief.

"Now come with me," said Narada.

When they reached the rabbit, his large family was by his side. Narada knelt down and gently removed the arrow. Mrigari watched in surprise as the rabbit's wound disappeared. The rabbit jumped high.

"Thank you, Sage," he said.

When they came to the boar, they found his children and wife surrounding him, their eyes red from crying. Again the sage removed the arrow, and the boar's wound healed.

Their tears of grief changed to tears of joy, and Mrigari felt happy inside.

Narada and Mrigari heard beautiful singing as they came near the fawn. She lay still while the birds and her mother sang to her. Mrigari began to cry.

He asked, "Sage, can you still save her?"

Narada placed his hands on the fawn to strengthen her. He whispered encouraging words in her ear. After a few minutes, he gently removed the arrow. Within moments her wound healed, and she awoke.

"You should have seen the celebration," the old man told his listeners. "All the animals cheered, singing and dancing around the fawn and her mother. And the love those animals had for Narada, you could see it in their eyes.

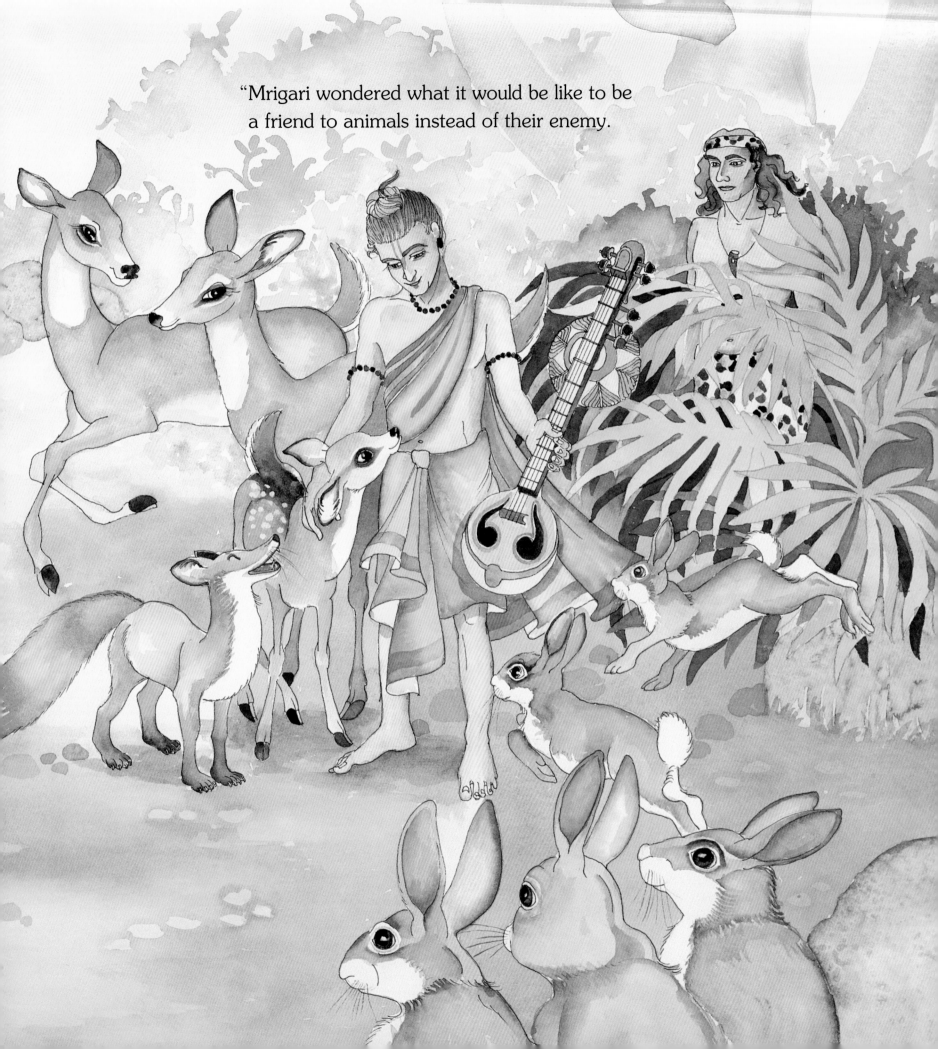

"Mrigari wondered what it would be like to be a friend to animals instead of their enemy.

"From that day on, the hunter became a new person. Narada's love and kindness changed that cruel hunter into a gentle, good-hearted man.

"I know, because I was the hunter."

The old man lowered his head.
A tear slid down his cheek.

Until that moment, the animals had only known the storyteller as a kind old man who shared his food with them, played with their young, and cared for their wounds. They saw his tears and gathered close to comfort him.

The buck spoke first. "Thank you for sharing your story with us. We will always remember it." The others nodded.

Then the smallest one of all, a young rabbit, jumped up onto the old man's lap. The other animals laughed. "I like your story," the rabbit said. "Your story gives me hope."

"Oh?" the old man asked, smiling. "What hope does it give you?"

In his biggest voice, so everyone could hear, the rabbit said, "Hope that other stories about hunters end as happily as this one."

NOTE TO TEACHERS AND PARENTS

THE PEACEABLE FOREST is a retelling of an ancient Vedic tale that has been passed on for centuries in the oral tradition from parents to children. This illustrated version of a beloved story from the Sanskrit Bhagavata Purana reminds children that compassion for living creatures and respect for life have their own rewards. The illustrations feature flora and fauna native to India, including langur monkeys, sarus cranes, and banyan and date palm trees.

ACKNOWLEDGMENTS

The author wishes to thank His Divine Grace A.C. Bhaktivedanta Swami
for his English translation of this story, originally published
in *The Teachings of Lord Caitanya* in 1968.

DEDICATED TO ALL THOSE WHO PRACTICE AHIMSA. —KOSA

TO THE WELFARE OF ALL ANIMALS ON OUR PLANET. —ANNA

INSIGHT KIDS
A MANDALA BOOK

PO Box 3088
San Rafael, CA 94912
www.insighteditions.com

Text copyright © 2012 Kosa Ely
Illustrations copyright © 2012 Anna Johansson

All rights reserved. No part of this book may be reproduced
in any form without written permission from the publisher.

Library of Congress Cataloging-in-Publication Data available.

ISBN: 978-1-60887-115-5

ROOTS of PEACE   REPLANTED PAPER

Insight Editions, in association with Roots of Peace, will plant two trees for each tree
used in the manufacturing of this book. Roots of Peace is an internationally renowned
humanitarian organization dedicated to eradicating land mines worldwide and
converting war-torn lands into productive farms and wildlife habitats. Together, we will
plant two million fruit and nut trees in Afghanistan and provide farmers there with the
skills and support necessary for sustainable land use.

Manufactured in China by Insight Editions

10 9 8 7 6 5 4 3 2 1